WHEN WILL I READ?

Miriam Cohen

Illustrated by Lillian Hoban

A Young Yearling Book

Published by
Dell Publishing
a division of
Bantam Doubleday Dell Publishing Group, Inc.
1540 Broadway
New York, New York 10036

ISBN: 0-440-49333-1

Reprinted by arrangement with Greenwillow Books, a division of William Morrow & Company, Inc.

Printed in the United States of America
November 1983
20 19 18 17 16 15 14 13
WES

To Dr. Jimmy Hymes,
Dr. Neith Headley,
Ruth Uhlmann,

and always
to Monroe

"When will I read?" Jim asked.
"Soon," the teacher said.

"But when?" said Jim.
"You know what the signs in
    our room say," the teacher said.

"Yes," said Jim. "I know
'Please put the blocks back
when you are done' and
'Don't let the hamsters out.'
But I always knew that."

"You can read your name,"
the teacher said.
"But that's not really reading," said Jim.
The teacher smiled. "It will happen,"
she said.
Then she went to get the snacks.

"I can read," George said.
"No, you can't," everybody shouted.
George took his favorite book
and told what it said under each picture.
"You only remembered it," Paul said.

"That's how reading begins,"
said the teacher. "It begins that way."

Anna Maria was reading to her baby
in the doll corner. She could really read.
"Quiet," she said. "I'm reading to you."
But her baby would not be quiet.

Anna Maria said, "Oh, this is a bad baby.
He needs to be washed."
And she began to wash her baby
very hard.

Jim said to Willy and Sammy,
"Everywhere there is reading. There is
reading about Smokey the Bear on the bus.
There is reading on the Nutty O's box.
Everywhere there is reading or writing,
writing or reading."

Willy said, "On the Nutty O's
box it tells you to send for
a little airplane."
"Yes," said Sammy. "I did.
But it crashed right away."

Jim sat down at the table.
He put his head on his arms.
"Don't worry," the teacher said.
"There's no hurry.
You will read
when you are ready."

"But when will I be ready?"
Jim asked.
"You are getting ready
all the time," she said.

Just then there was a cranking, bashing,
clashing noise outside the first grade windows.
"Let's go and watch the garbage men work,"
said the teacher.
The class rushed out to the playground.

The garbage men lifted the big cans
and dumped them into the truck.
The crunching teeth ate up the trash.
One of the garbage men winked at Jim.
He said, "How are you doing, son?"

Then the garbage men
jumped on the truck
and drove away,
waving and smiling
at the first grade.

Afterward the teacher wrote
down everybody's story
about the garbage men.

Here is Jim's.

Jim sat at the table, reading his story.
George and Willy and Sammy
sat down with him.
Jim said, "I wish I could really read."
"A dog can read," Sammy said.
"No, he can't!" everybody shouted.

"Yes, a dog can," said Sammy.
"He reads by the sniffs.
  He sniffs and then he knows
  which dog came there before."
"But can a dog read the comics?" asked
  George. Sammy and Willy fell down
  on the floor, laughing.

Jim was tired of worrying about reading.
He went to watch Danny and Paul and
Margaret. They were being firemen
and their block city was on fire.
Danny yelled, "Bring the water over here!"
"No," said Margaret. "We have to save this
man." She and Paul began to put up a ladder.

"Hurry!" Danny yelled.
"The fire is coming.
It will burn the hamsters."
He pretended to shoot water
on the hamsters' box.

Jim came to help Danny.
Then he saw that the sign
on the hamsters' box was torn.
It said, "Do let the hamsters out."

Jim ran to the teacher.
"Look!" he shouted.
"The sign says,
'Do let the hamsters out.'
They could get killed!"

"We can fix that!"
the teacher said.
And she began to
make a new sign.
Then she smiled at Jim.

"I told you it would happen,"
she said. "You can read."
"I can?" Jim said.
"Yes," said the teacher.
"That was reading.
You really read the sign."

Jim and the teacher put the new sign
on the hamsters' cage.
"I waited all my life," said Jim.
"Now I can read."